Little Kim's Doll

Text copyright © 1999 by Kim Yaroshevskaya
Illustrations copyright © 1999 by Luc Melanson

Groundwood Books / Douglas & McIntyre Ltd.
585 Bloor Street West, Toronto, Ontario M6G 1K5

Distributed in the USA by Publishers Group West
1700 Fourth Street, Berkeley, CA 94710

We acknowledge the financial support of the Canada Council for the Arts, the Ontario Arts Council and the Government of Canada through the Book Publishing Industry Development Program for our publishing activities.

Canadian Cataloguing in Publication data
Yaroshevskaya, Kim
[Petite Kim. English]
Little Kim's doll
"A Groundwood book."
Translation of: La petite Kim.
ISBN 0-88899-353-6
I. Title. II. Title: Petite Kim. English.
PS8597.A59P4713 1999   jC843'.54   C98-931955-5
PZ7.Y37Li 1999

Printed and bound in China

Story by Kim Yaroshevskaya

Little Kim's Doll

Pictures by Luc Melanson

A Groundwood Book

Douglas & McIntyre Toronto Vancouver Buffalo

There was once a very little girl
who lived in a big city
in a big country.
The name of the country was Russia,
the name of the city was Moscow,
and the little girl's name was Kim.

Her parents loved her dearly.
When they came home from work they brought
her presents:
a picture book
or building blocks
or a little pail and shovel to play with in the sand.

But what little Kim wanted more than
anything in the world
was a doll.

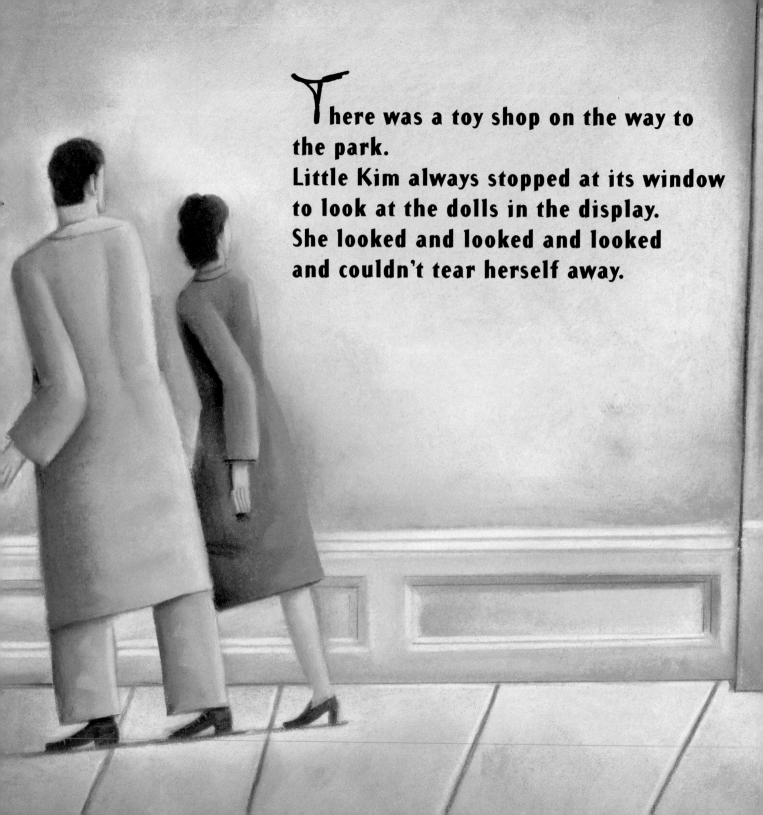

There was a toy shop on the way to
the park.
Little Kim always stopped at its window
to look at the dolls in the display.
She looked and looked and looked
and couldn't tear herself away.

One of the dolls was so perfect.
She was made of porcelain.
She had deep blue eyes
and braids the color of ripe wheat.

But little Kim's parents,
like many parents in Russia those days,
believed that little girls who played with dolls
would never learn to be brave and strong.

And since they wanted their little girl
to be among the bravest and the strongest,
they weren't going to buy her a doll. Ever.

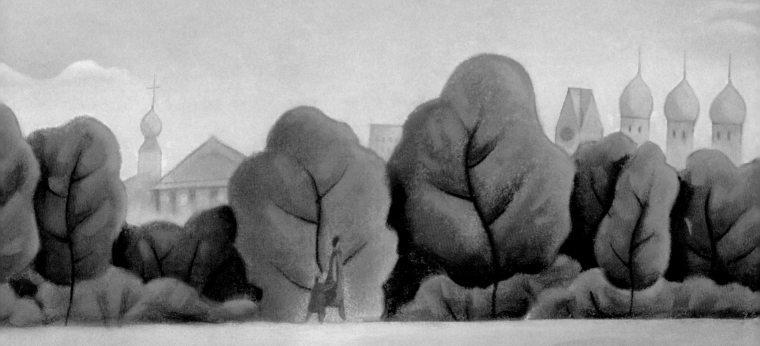

But little Kim wanted a doll.
And so, she found one.

It wasn't a real doll.
It was just an ordinary soup spoon.
Little Kim dressed it in a kerchief and called it Natasha.
She played with Natasha all day long.
She told Natasha stories, she ate with Natasha, she slept
with Natasha.

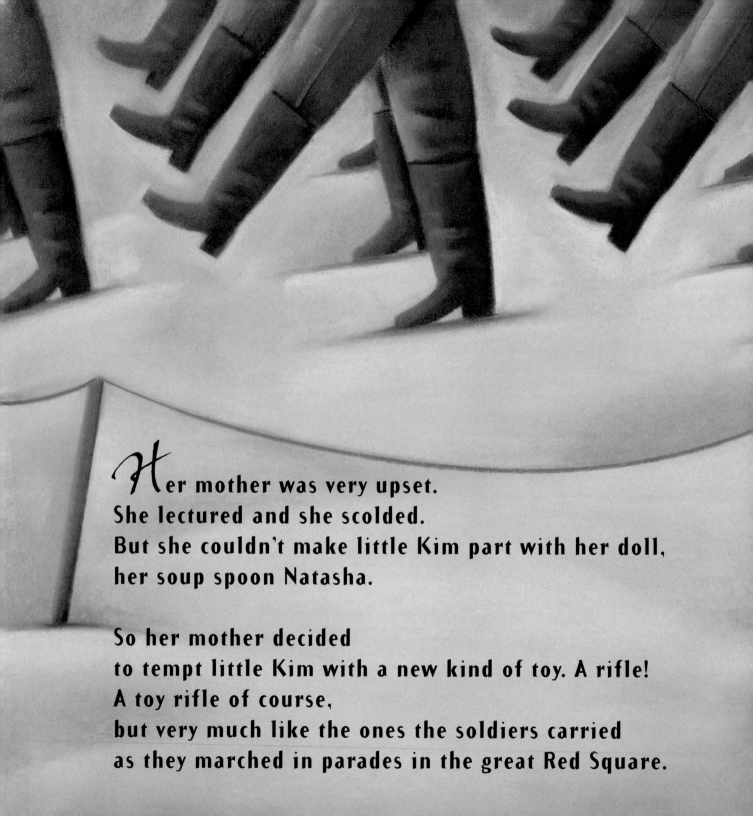

*H*er mother was very upset.
She lectured and she scolded.
But she couldn't make little Kim part with her doll,
her soup spoon Natasha.

So her mother decided
to tempt little Kim with a new kind of toy. A rifle!
A toy rifle of course,
but very much like the ones the soldiers carried
as they marched in parades in the great Red Square.

The rifle had a wooden handle shaped a little like a skirt.

Little Kim pressed the rifle to her heart.
She wrapped it in a cuddly blanket and rocked it gently,
singing a Russian lullaby:

> *Spi maliutka*
> *moy prekrasni*
> *baioushki-baiou...*

Her mother was furious!

But suddenly
a funny thought crossed her mind.
"Wait a minute," she said to herself.
"My little Kim goes on playing with her dolls
despite my anger and
despite my scolding.
That's what I call strength.
That's what I call courage!"

And then her mother smiled with pride.

On little Kim's next birthday,
the day she turned five years old,
there was a doll among her presents!

She was a porcelain doll.
She had deep blue eyes
and braids the color of ripe wheat.

And there wasn't a happier little girl
in the whole world!